Stories of the Nibelungen

Edited by Gertrude R. Schottenfels

Illustrated by John C. Gilbert

Cover Art by Arthur Rackham

Copyright © 2013 Granny's Attic Press

All rights reserved.

ISBN-13: 978-1490965970
ISBN-10: 1490965971

First published in 1905 as:

Stories of the Nibelungen for Young People

CONTENTS

1	Young Siegfried	1
2	Mimi's Story	7
3	Siegfried's Sword	12
4	The Death of the Dragon	16
5	The Story of Brunhilda	20
6	Gunther and Kriemhild	24
7	Siegfried's Return to Ireland	28
8	How Gunther Won His Bride	31
9	Kriemhild and Brunhilda's Quarrel	35
10	Kriemhild's Revenge	43

1

YOUNG SIEGFRIED

In the good old days of Long Ago, when kings had absolute power over all their subjects, even in the matter of life and death, there dwelt in the city of Santum, on the beautiful Rhine River, a great and good king named Siegmund.

He was very powerful, and ruled over the kingdom of Niederland so wisely and so well that he was loved and honored by all his people. He shared his throne with Siegelinda, his beautiful wife, who also was noble and kind of heart.

Siegmund and Siegelinda had one son, called Siegfried—a handsome, well-built lad, with eyes as blue and sunny as the sky above on a fair spring morning. He was the only child of the king and queen, but he was more of a sorrow than a joy to them, for he was as willful and disobedient as he was beautiful. He could not bear to be crossed in any way, and wished that he were a man, so that he might do exactly as he pleased.

Siegfried's parents loved him dearly in spite of his faults and all the sorrow his wild ways caused them. But one fine morning, while the king and queen were still asleep, he quietly took his hat, and stole out of the castle, for he had made up his mind to go out into the wide world to seek his fortune.

Siegfried walked through the beautiful city, and then for some time followed a winding country road, until at length he found himself in the midst of a dense forest. But he was not afraid; he could hear the birds singing and calling to one another in the green trees overhead, and now and then a rabbit or a timid squirrel ran across his pathway, and disappeared in the bushes.

So he wandered along, quite happy. Sometimes he would come to a little brook, winding its way through the trees and grass, and babbling and singing among its pebbles. Across the stream he would leap, as lightly as a hare.

Thus the day wore on, and as twilight gathered, he began to feel very tired and hungry. He was just beginning to wonder what he should do, when he noticed that he was nearing the edge of the forest, and a little farther on what should he see but a blacksmith's shop among the bushes.

In the doorway stood the smith himself in his leathern apron—a little, odd, misshapen dwarf named Mimi. He looked in wonder at the beautiful boy, who smiled upon him in a friendly way, and said:

"Good-evening. I am almost dead with thirst and hunger; will you not take me in, and let me be your helper?"

Mimi was about to say no, when he chanced to look at Siegfried the second time. He noticed how strong and well built the boy was; so he said:

"I am not really in need of a helper, for in this out-of-the-way place there is very little work to be done; but if you wish to learn my trade, I am willing to give you a trial."

Siegfried was happy to hear this, and with a hearty relish he ate the coarse brown bread and bowl of milk which Mimi brought to him.

The next morning the blacksmith showed Siegfried how to blow the bellows, and swing the sledge-hammer, and also how to shape a horseshoe.

"Now, you try it," he said, laying a red-hot piece of iron on the anvil.

Siegfried was eager to try. He raised the hammer above his head, and brought it down with such force that the iron flew to pieces and the anvil was buried in the ground.

Mimi was very angry. He gave the boy a box on the ear that nearly knocked him over. Now, Siegfried was a king's son, and never before in all his life had any one but his parents dared to punish him. Therefore he was indignant, and without giving Mimi a moment's warning, he seized the dwarf by the collar and dashed him to the ground.

When Mimi came to his senses, he was almost dead with pain and fright. He made up his mind then and there that he would have his revenge, but he knew he was no match for Siegfried in strength; so he picked himself up, and pretended that he was not in the least angry. After a while he sent Siegfried to fetch a basket of coal from the colliery, which was near a great linden tree in the forest.

THE MEETING OF SIEGFRIED AND MIMI

Under this tree dwelt a terrible monster, and Mimi hoped that the huge beast would make an end of the lad.

As Siegfried reached the tree, out rushed the monster, with open jaws, ready to devour him. But the boy nimbly sprang aside, and uprooting a tree which stood near, he brought it down with such force on the monster's back that the huge creature was dazed by the blow, and lay writhing in pain.

Then quick as thought, Siegfried pulled up tree after tree, and piled them high above the struggling monster, pinning him fast to the earth. Thus he slowly crushed the terrible beast to death.

As he stood there watching, a pool of blood oozed slowly out from under the pile of trees. He dipped his finger in it without thinking, and was surprised and delighted to find that his finger had become as hard as horn, and that he could neither scratch nor pierce it.

"What a fine thing!" thought the lad. "I will bathe myself in the pool, and then nothing on earth can harm me."

Accordingly, he quickly undressed and bathed himself in the pool; but as he was stooping over, a broad leaf from the linden tree fell upon his back, between the shoulders, and the spot where it lay was not touched by the monster's blood. Siegfried knew nothing of the leaf. "Now," said he to himself, "I am safe; neither sword nor spear can wound me." Then he cut off the monster's head, filled Mimi's basket with coal, and carried both back to the smithy.

Mimi could hardly believe his eyes when Siegfried appeared; he began to fear the wonderful strength of this half-grown boy, and to hate him with a deadly hatred.

However, he was far too wise to let Siegfried know his feelings, and so he praised the lad's courage highly. But he at once began to think of another plan to get rid of him.

That night, while they were sitting together before the fire, Mimi said:

"I know of an adventure which would just suit you, Siegfried. If you succeed in it, it will make you famous all over the world, and you will be very rich."

The boy was eager to be off at once, but the dwarf declared that Siegfried must first listen to a long, strange story. Mimi bade him give good heed to what he was about to hear.

2

MIMI'S STORY

My father was a dwarf, and belonged to a race of dwarfs called the Nibelungs. He had three sons, Fafner, Otto, and myself. Fafner was the eldest; I was the youngest. Otto, my second brother, was very fond of fishing, and liked nothing better than to spend whole days at the sport.

My father had a magic cap called a tarnhelm. Any one who put this cap on could make himself invisible, or assume any form he desired. Otto would borrow this tarnhelm, and assuming the form of an otter, he would go to a waterfall near our home to fish. He would go right into the water, and catching the fish in his mouth, would lay them down on the bank, one after another, until he had enough. Then he would become himself once more and would carry the fish home for supper.

Near this waterfall there lived another dwarf, named Alberich, who also belonged to the race of the Nibelungs. He possessed a great treasure of gold, which he had captured from the nymphs of the Rhine. The father of the nymphs, the God of the Rhine, had entrusted the treasure to their care.

Alberich gained possession of the Rhine gold, but in doing so he lost everything which helps to make life beautiful. Like my brother, he was very fond of fishing, and taking the form of a huge pike, he would go with Otto to the waterfall, and fish all day.

One day Wotan, the King of the Gods, was wandering through the forest with Loki, the God of Fire. They were both very tired and hungry, and as they came near the waterfall, what should they spy but an otter in the water, with a large salmon in its mouth. Here was a chance not to be missed.

Seizing a big stone, Loki hurled it with all his might at the otter, killing it instantly. Then they carried it to my father's house, and begged for a night's lodging.

As soon as my father saw the otter, he told them that they had killed his son. Both Wotan and Loki were very sorry to hear this, and regretted that they could not restore my brother to life. To make up to my father for what they had done, they agreed to fill the otter skin with gold, and also to cover the outside of it with the same precious metal. Then Wotan sent Loki out in search of gold.

Now Loki knew that the dwarf Alberich possessed the Rhine gold; so he hastened to the waterfall, and demanded the entire treasure.

At first Alberich refused to part with the gold; but Loki threatened to kill him unless he gave it up. So Alberich unwillingly gave the treasure to Loki—all except a ring of gold, which he kept hidden in his hand. But the god's eyes were sharp, and he saw what Alberich had done.

Now this ring was a magic ring, and whoever owned it might claim all the gold in all the rivers and mountains upon earth. Alberich believed that if he kept it he could some day get back his treasure through its magic power.

Loki commanded him to give it up, and the dwarf refused to do so. Seeing that words were useless, the god snatched it from Alberich's hand, and started off. Alberich fell into a terrible fury, and cried:

"A curse upon the gold! Death to all its possessors!"

But Loki had obtained that which he set out to get. The gold was not to be his, and he cared nothing for the dwarf and his curses. He only laughed at Alberich, and hastened with his burden to my father's house.

When Wotan saw the gold ring, he was so pleased with its beauty that he placed it on his finger, intending to keep it for himself. Then they filled the otter's skin with gold, and also covered it over, according to their promise. When they had finished, my father discovered one spot on its head upon which there was no gold. He insisted upon having this covered up, and since there was no more gold to be had, Wotan unwillingly took the ring from his finger, and placed it there.

Loki was displeased, and cried:

"Now, you ingrate, you have the most enormous gold treasure in the world, and I hope you are satisfied! But remember what I say: The gold will prove your ruin, and it will also cause your son to fill an early grave."

"FLEE FOR YOUR LIFE ERE I SMITE YOU DEAD"

Then the gods took their departure.

Fafner and I asked our father to give us each a share of the gold; but he only laughed in a disagreeable way, and declared his dead son was far more precious to him than were his living sons. He said that every hair on Otto's head was dear to him. Then he ran after us with a stone club, and swore that he would kill us if we said another word. We said no more, and crept away in fear.

But that night as my father lay asleep, Fafner stole into his room and slew him. Then I came forward, and told my brother that I had witnessed his evil deed, and demanded that he give me half of the gold. But he turned upon me in a blind rage, and cried:

"Flee for your life ere I smite you dead!"

I fled in fear, without another word. Then Fafner put on my father's tarnhelm and escaped with his treasure to the heath, where he hid it in a cave among the rocks. But, fearful lest it be taken from him, he assumed the form of a frightful dragon, that he might protect it better.

And there he lies day and night, guarding the entrance of the cave, and leaves it only when he goes to drink at a neighboring spring. No one has dared attack him, for no one has the strength to match him.

3

SIEGFRIED'S SWORD

When Mimi had finished his story, he looked at Siegfried, who had been drinking in every word with breathless interest, and asked:

"Well, my lad, what do you think of that? Do you think you could kill the dragon?"

Siegfried answered, with shining eyes:

"Come, Mimi, forge me a mighty sword, and lead the way to Fafner's cave, and I will show you what I can do."

So Mimi set to work to fashion a sword for Siegfried. It was to be the strongest, sharpest one that man had ever made. The dwarf worked day and night until it was finished.

When he gave it to Siegfried, the boy examined it carefully, shook his head as though in doubt, and then strode to the anvil. He struck the iron one powerful blow with the sword, and the weapon lay in pieces.

Mimi told him not to worry, and at once set to work upon some of his most finely tempered steel, resolved to make a sword that would be a match for Siegfried's unheard-of strength.

But when it was finished, Siegfried took it as he had taken the first, and in a moment the blade was shattered on the anvil. Then he grew angry and rushed at the dwarf, crying:

"Oh! you worthless fellow, get you hence or I will kill you!"

Mimi was badly frightened, and hid himself behind the fireplace not knowing what might happen next. But after a while Siegfried's anger began to cool; then Mimi emerged from his hiding-place, and Siegfried saw that he held something in each hand. When the dwarf came close enough, the lad saw that he carried two halves of a splendid sword.

This Mimi declared was none other than the sword Wotan had carried on the day upon which Otto was killed. "And," he continued, "if I can but weld it together, you will have the finest sword that ever a hero wielded." Siegfried could scarcely wait until Mimi finished the work, so anxious was he to try the weapon.

At length it was ready, and he seized it, crying: "Now for the test! Now for the test!" Then he raised the mighty blade high above his head, and brought it down with all his strength upon the anvil. The whole house shook and trembled, and the anvil was split in two, but the weapon—the mighty sword that Wotan himself had flourished—was unhurt.

And now Mimi was thoroughly frightened, for he thought that Siegfried must be Thor himself. But he hid his fear, and cried:

"Avenge me, Siegfried! Slay this dragon, and one-half of the Rhine gold shall be yours."

"Lead the way," the lad replied, "and I will make short work of him."

So Mimi started for the heath, and Siegfried followed him joyfully.

When they drew near the place, Mimi pointed out a wide, blackened trail leading through the grass. This, he said, had been made by Fafner, for it was the path the dragon took each day when he went to the spring to drink. The dwarf told the boy that Fafner spouted flames to the right and left as he went along, and threshed the grass with his monstrous tail at every step.

Then he advised Siegfried to dig a deep pit, hide himself in it, and as the dragon crawled over it, to pierce him to the heart from underneath. Siegfried thought the plan a good one, and proceeded at once to dig.

He did not hear Mimi chuckling to himself, behind his back. For Mimi was bent upon destroying him, and knew that as soon as he had killed the monster, its blood would fill the pit, and drown him. Therefore the dwarf rejoiced. He withdrew to a safe distance, and hid himself, to await the coming of the dragon, which he greatly feared.

THE MIGHTY SWORD WAS UNHURT

4

THE DEATH OF THE DRAGON

As Siegfried was digging, he became aware of a tall one-eyed stranger, clad in a long gray cloak, who was standing near by, watching him intently. The stranger inquired what Siegfried was doing, and upon being told, earnestly advised the youth to dig several pits, each opening out of the other, so that he might escape the flow of blood which would otherwise drown him.

Siegfried was very grateful for the advice, and began to act upon it at once. Then Wotan (for the one-eyed stranger was none other than the god) disappeared from view. When he was through digging, Siegfried heaped brush and weeds above the first pit, so that it might not be noticed, and getting down into it, awaited the coming of the dragon.

He had not long to wait. Of a sudden, a great noise, like the tramping of a thousand horses, fell upon his ear. Then came a roaring as of the sea, and he saw the huge monster come slowly along, thrashing the earth with its great tail, and spouting flames to the left and the right.

On and on it came, until he could feel its breath hot above his face. He firmly grasped his sword, and gave one swift upward thrust, quickly withdrawing it, and then he nimbly leaped into the next pit, followed by a rush of blood, and then through the next, and so on, till he reached safe ground.

When he went back to the first pit, he found the dragon writhing and groaning in its death agony. As soon as it saw him, it cried out, for it still retained the power of human speech:

"Oh! you unlucky one, the gold will prove your ruin as it has mine. A curse is on it. Who has it is accursed!"

Saying this, the creature died.

Then Siegfried carefully cleaned his sword, and replaced it in its sheath, and as he did so, he noticed some blood upon his hand. He licked it off, and no sooner had it touched his tongue, than a strange thing happened. He could understand everything which the birds overhead were saying. He stood still and listened, and what was his astonishment to find that they were actually talking to him!

One told him that Mimi was untrue to him, and was constantly plotting his death; that even at that very moment the dwarf was approaching with a poisoned drink which he would offer to Siegfried, so that he might not have to keep his promise of sharing the Rhine gold. The bird advised him to kill the dwarf.

Sure enough, at that very moment Mimi came forward, praising Siegfried's bravery, and offering him the poisoned drink in the most friendly manner, smiling deceitfully all the while. Our hero turned upon him in anger, and forced him to drain the cup himself, whereupon the wretched dwarf fell to earth, lifeless.

"THE GOLD WILL PROVE YOUR RUIN!"

Then the birds told Siegfried to enter the dragon's cave, and get the ring and the tarnhelm, the possession of which would make him all-powerful. This he did, and then he rolled the dragon's enormous body to the entrance of the cave, where the Rhine gold still lay, and sealed up the entrance with it.

As he stood there, wondering what he should do next, he heard the birds singing of a mountain far away, where a maiden named Brunhilda lay in an enchanted sleep, surrounded by a ring of magic flames. Here she must slumber till there should appear a man strong and brave enough to dash through the flames and waken her with a kiss.

Siegfried determined to journey to the mountain. So he returned to the smithy, and saddled Mimi's horse, which was a strong, faithful creature, and then he rode away to seek the sleeping maiden.

Many days and nights he wandered, and at length, early one morning as he ascended the highlands, he saw a rosy glow in the distance, which grew ever brighter and brighter. "The rising sun," he said to himself, but he knew that it was not the rising sun. On and on he rode, and ever brighter and brighter grew the sky, until at length he came upon the flames themselves, and he knew that he had reached his journey's end.

5

THE STORY OF BRUNHILDA

As Siegfried drew nearer, he could hear the crackling of the flames, and when his horse saw the fire, the animal reared up on its hind legs, and snorted in terror. But Siegfried knew no fear. Putting spurs to his horse, he boldly forced it through the flames, and, lo! both horse and rider passed through unharmed.

Before Siegfried's eyes was a wondrous sight. On the mountain stood a castle, the strangest ever seen, for it was built entirely of green marble, as were all the buildings round it; and there, on the grassy slope before the castle, lay a young warrior, clad in shining armor, with a helmet on his head.

Siegfried went up to him, to ask him where he might find the maiden. But the warrior was sunk in slumber, and made no reply when Siegfried spoke. Siegfried shook him roughly, to waken him, but he still slept on. Then Siegfried opened the young man's visor and removed his helmet. What was his surprise to find, within, the long fair hair and rosy face of a beautiful woman!

This, then, was Brunhilda; it could be no other. Bending over her, he pressed a kiss lightly on her lips.

Immediately Brunhilda awoke, and thanked the young hero for breaking the magic spell which bound her. Then, as they sat together in the marble palace, Brunhilda told her story.

She was one of Wotan's eight daughters who were called Walkyries. They were beautiful goddesses of immense size and strength, and used to follow Wotan when he went into battle. Occasionally, when two knights or two countries battled against each other, they would award the palm of victory to one or the other. It was also their duty to carry all slain heroes to Walhalla, the beautiful palace of Wotan.

One day Brunhilda disobeyed her father's orders, and awarded the victory to the hero whom Wotan wished overthrown. Wotan was very angry, and as a punishment he forbade her to dwell among the gods and goddesses, and declared that never again should she set foot in Walhalla. Furthermore, he would cause her to wed a mortal man, thus becoming a mortal woman, instead of a goddess.

Brunhilda was overcome with grief, as were all of her sisters. They all pleaded with Wotan not to punish her in this way. But he had already pronounced sentence upon her, and could not retract his word. Then Brunhilda wept piteously, and begged him at least to grant that her husband might be a hero. This he promised, and then disclosed his plan.

PUTTING SPURS TO HIS HORSE, HE BOLDLY
FORCED IT THROUGH THE FLAMES

He would sink her in a magic sleep, and would order Loki, the fire-god, to kindle some magic flames, which were to encircle her. She was to slumber until awakened by a man brave enough to go through fire for her sake. "And," continued Wotan, "of course only a hero would show such courage." Then he assured her that when the hero came he should be unharmed by the ring of fire.

And so, with streaming eyes, Brunhilda bade her sisters a long farewell. Never again, so long as she lived, would she behold them. Wotan was deeply touched when he saw her grief, and with a last tender kiss upon her beautiful brow, he laid her on the grassy slope, and pronounced the magic words which bound her.

6

GUNTHER AND KRIEMHILD

Siegfried remained for a long time with Brunhilda at Isenheim (which was the ancient name for Ireland), where all the buildings were of green marble. He then started for home, promising her that he would return and marry her, as soon as he had visited his parents, whom he now felt he had treated very cruelly.

Brunhilda replied that she too thought that he ought to visit his mother and father, but that he must promise to return as soon as he had done so. He readily promised, and sealed his pledge by placing his magic ring upon her finger. Then he set out for Niederland.

On the way thither, he had to pass through the city of Worms in Burgundy. Now in this city dwelt a powerful king called Gunther, who ruled over all Burgundy. He had an uncle named Hagen, who was his dead father's brother, and who was also Gunther's most valued adviser on all occasions. Gunther was so great and mighty that four and twenty kings paid him tribute.

He had a sister, named Kriemhild, who was noted far and wide for her wondrous beauty. Once Kriemhild had had a strange dream: She thought that she was out hunting with her pet falcon, and that two fierce eagles swooped down from the sky, and killed the bird before her eyes.

Now in these olden times people were very superstitious, and believed that every dream had a meaning. Kriemhild related her dream to her mother, Uota, and asked what it meant. Uota replied:

"The falcon signifies a noble man who will win you for his bride; but the two eagles stand for two powerful enemies, who will cause his death."

Then Kriemhild was very sad, and declared that she did not wish to marry any one, as it would bring her only sorrow.

Not long after this Siegfried arrived at Worms, and although he knew no one in all the city, everybody was anxious to learn who he was, he was so handsome and noble looking. Hagen advised Gunther to make friends with him, for he thought it very likely that the stranger might prove to be Siegfried, whose fame was spreading fast.

Hagen related how Siegfried had killed the linden-monster, slain the dragon, won the Rhine gold, and gained possession of the magic cap and ring. When Uota heard all this, she determined that Siegfried should marry her beautiful daughter. When he entered the castle at Worms, Gunther received him cordially, and made haste to offer him both food and drink. Siegfried accepted both gratefully, for he was hungry and thirsty. Uota hastily prepared a magic potion, and no sooner had the hero drunk it than all memory of the past, Brunhilda included, faded from his mind.

UOTA GIVES SIEGFRIED THE MAGIC POTION

Siegfried remained at Worms for one whole year, and in all that time he never once got a glimpse of Kriemhild, although the fame of her beauty reached him from every side. She, however, had seen him from her window while he was tilting with her brother's knights, and she thought that never before had she seen any one so brave and handsome.

Not long after this, the Danes and the Saxons declared war against Gunther. He quickly gathered together his army, and set out to battle with them. His two younger brothers, Giselherr and Gernot, went with him, and Siegfried accompanied him as his body-guard.

And now began anxious days and nights for Kriemhild. She was filled with dread lest her brothers or Siegfried be slain. She eagerly awaited tidings of every battle. She heard that the Saxons and Danes were being hard pressed, and also that the most brave and reckless warrior among all the Burgundian hosts was her brother's guest and body-guard.

Not long after this, the Burgundians were victorious, and captured both the Danish and the Saxon king. This ended the war, and Gunther and all his troops returned to Worms, where the king held a great feast to celebrate his victory. And here for the first time Siegfried saw Kriemhild, and he thought her the most beautiful woman he had ever seen.

He was almost afraid to speak to her, so wondrous was her beauty, but she thanked him very prettily and gratefully for all that he had done for her brother; and when he replied that everything he had done had been done for her sake, she smiled and was content. Siegfried had fallen deeply in love with her, and made up his mind to spare no effort to win her for his bride.

7

SIEGFRIED RETURNS TO IRELAND

Meanwhile, in Ireland, Brunhilda was eagerly awaiting Siegfried's return. Days grew into weeks, weeks lengthened into months, and still he did not come. At first she could not believe that he had deserted her. She would look at the beautiful ring which he had given her, and all her faith and trust in him would return.

But when months slowly lengthened into years, and the years passed one after another, she began to give up the hope of ever seeing him again.

Now, as I have said before, Brunhilda was very beautiful, and soon suitors began flocking around her, anxious to win her hand in marriage. But Brunhilda loved Siegfried very dearly and had no desire to marry any one else. Therefore she declared that whoever sought to marry her must match his strength with hers; if he were victorious, she would wed him, but if he failed, he should lose his head in forfeit, according to the custom of these olden days.

Many gallant suitors came, entered the contest, failed and lost their heads, for Brunhilda was a Walkyrie, and more than a match in strength for any man. She did not like to kill her lovers, but they persisted in coming, and she continued to do her best at every trial.

Meanwhile the fame of her strength and beauty traveled afar, and reached Gunther at Worms. He determined to journey to Isenheim, and enter the lists against her. Accordingly he went to Siegfried, and asked aid of him. Siegfried replied:

"I will gladly help you, if you, on your part, will help me win the hand of your beautiful sister."

Gunther was very grateful for the aid Siegfried had given him in the late Saxon war. So he promised that on the day Brunhilda arrived in Worms he would give him Kriemhild for his bride. Siegfried was satisfied, and agreed to travel to Ireland with Gunther, as his vassal, and to present his petition to Brunhilda.

Then they arrayed themselves in costly garments and set sail, and after a twelve-day voyage, they reached the coast of Ireland. When Siegfried beheld the green palaces of marble, he felt a vague uneasiness, for it all had a strangely familiar look. Where had he seen this place before? He remembered it dimly, as in a dream.

When he entered Brunhilda's palace, she advanced to meet him, with both hands outstretched, crying:

"Siegfried, is it indeed you, and have you come to tilt with me?"

He looked at her with the eyes of a stranger, and replied:

"I come to represent Gunther, King of Burgundy. He wishes to sue for your heart and hand. He is my lord; I am his vassal, and have come to do his bidding."

Brunhilda was sorely grieved and perplexed; she could not in the least understand Siegfried's behavior. Surely it was he who had aroused her from her magic sleep, and surely it was he who had placed the beautiful ring upon her hand, vowing that he would return and claim her for his bride. But as he continued to look at her as though he had never seen her before, she felt that she must give him a reply.

And as she had no reasonable excuse for refusing his request, she said that Gunther might enter the lists with her. She felt sure that he, too, would be overthrown. Siegfried thanked her gravely for her kindness, and made haste to carry her reply back to Gunther.

He then disclosed his plan to aid Gunther in the undertaking. Gunther was to appear clad in armor and mounted upon Siegfried's horse, the one which had belonged to Mimi; then he, Siegfried, would put on his tarnhelm and become invisible; Gunther was to ride boldly into the field, and go through all the necessary motions, while Siegfried, unseen by the others, would do all the actual fighting. Gunther said he considered the plan a capital one, and declared that Siegfried was as clever as he was brave.

8

HOW GUNTHER WON HIS BRIDE

The day of the tournament dawned bright and fair. The field was crowded with lovely women and brave knights. Twelve men now appeared, bearing an immense round stone, which was so large that it took all their united strength to handle it. They set it down in that part of the field where the contest was to take place.

At length all was ready. From the castle issued forth the warrior-king and the warrior-maiden. They were clad in glistening armor, and mounted on prancing chargers. The signal was given, and then began a test of strength such as had never before been witnessed.

Brunhilda seized her javelin, and hurled it with such force that when Siegfried caught it upon Gunther's shield the shield was shattered into pieces. Then Siegfried, still invisible, grasped Gunther's javelin, and hurled it with such force at Brunhilda that she was thrown to the ground. She was overcome with surprise and anger; never before had such a thing befallen her.

Quickly recovering herself, she sprang to her feet, and grasping the huge stone which twelve men had found hard to carry, she whirled it deftly thrice around her head, and then threw it far into the distance. Then, while the people sat spell-bound, she leaped after it, and sprang lightly over the stone.

"Now," thought she to herself, "surely no one can do more than that."

But she had reckoned without Siegfried. Hastily seizing the stone, he hurled it much farther than Brunhilda had thrown it, and not to be outdone by her, he grasped Gunther firmly under the arms, and sprang with him over the stone, landing much farther beyond it than she had.

Then a mighty shout from thousands of throats rent the air, and while the people were crowding around, hailing Gunther as victor, Siegfried tore off his tarnhelm, and took his place among the crowd.

And now what could Brunhilda do? She had publicly proclaimed that she would marry any man whose strength was greater than her own, so sure had she felt of her power. She would not break her word, and so with a sorrowful heart she made ready to travel back to Worms with Gunther.

At Worms Kriemhild joyfully accepted Siegfried's hand, and there was a grand double wedding, at which all Burgundy was present. The festivities lasted fourteen days.

One evening, while Gunther and his bride were sitting together, Gunther noticed tears on Brunhilda's lashes, and asked what was troubling her. She replied that she was grieving that his sister had married his vassal. This was not the truth. She was feeling sad and lonely because the man she loved so well had taken Kriemhild for his bride.

BRUNHILDA WAS THROWN TO THE GROUND

Gunther told her not to worry, as he could explain all that to her, and promised to do so at some future time. He said that Siegfried was greater than she knew.

After the wedding, Siegfried and Kriemhild journeyed to Santum, to visit Siegmund and Siegelinda, whom he had left in his youth. They were overjoyed to see him, and listened with breathless interest to all he had to tell. They knew all about the dragon, and the Rhine gold, and the magic cap which he had won, for the fame of his wondrous deeds had traveled far and wide. And now, strange to tell, Siegfried had recovered the memory of almost all his past; only Brunhilda and the magic ring remained forgotten.

After the young couple had been at Santum for some time, Siegmund withdrew from his throne, and made Siegfried and Kriemhild the rulers of the kingdom. The people of Niederland hailed the hero with delight, although they grieved to give up their old king and queen, who had won the hearts of all their subjects by their wisdom and kindness.

9

KRIEMHILD AND BRUNHILDA'S QUARREL

Years passed by, and Brunhilda had come to love her husband very dearly. They had one child, a little boy whom they had named Siegfried. Kriemhild, meanwhile, had been living very happily with her husband in Niederland. They had had two great sorrows, the death of the old king and that of the queen, and all the people of Niederland still mourned the loss of these two.

Then there arrived one day in Niederland a messenger from the King and Queen of Burgundy, inviting Siegfried and Kriemhild to attend a great feast which was to be held in Worms. They accepted with pleasure. Kriemhild was anxious to see her mother and brothers again, for she loved them dearly. So they started for Burgundy.

For some days after they arrived in Worms everything went happily. But then the tournaments began, and Siegfried won every honor as he had done in days gone by, for he had lost none of his wonderful strength. Both the queens were present at the contests, and as he overthrew one knight after another, Kriemhild looked at him lovingly, and said that he was the best and greatest king the world had ever seen, and that no king could stand against him; all paid him tribute.

Brunhilda replied: "All except Gunther; next to him Siegfried is the most powerful king on earth; but strong as your husband is, he could never hold his own against Gunther."

Kriemhild controlled her temper, and made no reply, but that evening when they attended vespers, Kriemhild attempted to enter the cathedral first. Brunhilda interfered, saying:

"The wife of a vassal should never precede the wife of his lord!"

"And who says that King Siegfried is Gunther's vassal?" demanded Kriemhild.

"I have his own word for it," Brunhilda replied. "When they first appeared in Ireland, Siegfried approached me, saying: 'I come to represent the King of Burgundy; I am his vassal, he is my lord.'"

Then Kriemhild lost all patience, for well she knew by what trick Gunther had won his bride. She cried:

"And do you think that Gunther overthrew you in the tilt? Gunther only pretended to fight. It was Siegfried, made invisible by his tarnhelm, who did the real fighting; it was Siegfried who hurled the javelin which unhorsed you; it was Siegfried who threw the heavy stone, and he it was, invisible to you, but holding Gunther in his arms, who sprang over the stone, and vanquished you," she declared.

Looking at Kriemhild's heaving breast and blazing eye, Brunhilda knew she spoke the truth. And at the same time, there flashed across her mind something that Gunther had once said to her about Siegfried being greater than she knew.

And now she fell into a royal rage, and her indignation knew no bounds. There was but one way of atonement; Siegfried must die for the deceit practiced on her. So she went to Hagen, Gunther's uncle, who had promised always to defend her rights, and demanded Siegfried's life.

When Hagen first spoke to Gunther of the matter, Gunther would not hear of the plan to do away with Siegfried, and vowed that no harm should befall the man with whom he had sworn blood brothership ere they set out for Ireland. But Brunhilda was firm in her resolve; nothing less than his death would satisfy her honor, nor wipe out the stain of his deceit.

And finally Gunther gave an unwilling consent. However, they could not fall upon Siegfried, and kill him in cold blood, so Hagen made a clever plan: they would receive a false summons to war. Accordingly, a few days later, a messenger rode posthaste into Worms, bearing the false tidings that the enemy was approaching.

Then everything was in great confusion, and Gunther assembled his hosts, and set out to meet the enemy. Siegfried accompanied him, to render what assistance he could, for he loved his kinsman as a brother. Just before the army started on the march, Kriemhild went to Hagen, and begged him to watch over her husband, and see to it that no one attacked him from behind, for she explained that Siegfried could not be wounded anywhere except in the spot on his back where the linden-leaf had fallen.

"IT WAS SIEGFRIED WHO DID THE REAL FIGHTING"

Hagen readily promised. He craftily suggested that Kriemhild should sew some mark above the spot, so that he might know exactly when danger threatened. Kriemhild fell in at once with his plan; with loving care she stitched a white silk cross upon her husband's clothes. Then Gunther and his troops rode away.

After they had ridden some distance, they were met by another messenger, with the false tidings that the enemy had begun a retreat.

Gunther appeared to be overjoyed at the news, and suggested that a mighty hunt should be held, to celebrate the occasion. The troops were dispatched back to Worms, and the royal party set out for the chase, which they greatly enjoyed.

When the dinner-horn sounded for the hunters to assemble to their meal, Siegfried appeared, dragging a live bear behind him. He was received with shouts of applause. They at once proceeded to kill and roast the bear. Every one was in the best of spirits, and as hungry as could be; but when they sat down to eat, it was discovered that the wine was missing; Hagen had purposely left it behind.

Siegfried, especially, was very thirsty, and playfully chided Hagen for forgetting so important an article. Thereupon Hagen said that he knew of a spring, not far away, where Siegfried might quench his thirst, and dared him to run a race there. Siegfried accepted the challenge, and easily won the race, as Hagen knew he would.

He had laid aside his weapons, and was already kneeling to drink, when Hagen came up behind him. "Ha, ha," laughed Siegfried, "I have won the race, and am therefore entitled to the first drink."

"You are," answered Hagen quietly, picking up Siegfried's sword, and poising it above the spot where Kriemhild had sewn the white cross; and without saying another word, he drove it home with such force that the point of it pierced Siegfried's breast.

In agony, the hero sprang to his feet, and seizing his shield, hurled it with all his might at Hagen, throwing him to the ground. Then he, too, fell, and the blood from his wounds stained the grass a deep crimson; and thus died Siegfried, the great and mighty hero, calling upon Kriemhild with his last breath to avenge his foul murder.

Then they placed his body on his shield and carried it back to Worms, and laid it at Kriemhild's door. Next morning, as she was going to mass, her waiting-maid, who preceded her on the way out, suddenly gave a scream, and cried:

"Go back, go back, and do not come this way, for here lies the body of a dead warrior."

But Kriemhild's heart misgave her, and she would not go back, and when she saw the body she uttered a great cry, for she knew instantly that it was Siegfried.

She bade the servants carry it inside, and lay it on his bed, and her grief knew no bounds. Then she sent for Gunther, and wildly accused him of the deed, and he as wildly denied his guilt. Then she said:

"If you are indeed innocent, you need not fear to stand in the presence of the dead."

"THE HERO HURLED IT WITH ALL HIS MIGHT AT HAGEN"

Gunther was not afraid, and went with her into the death chamber. While they were standing there, looking at Siegfried, Hagen suddenly entered the room, and lo! all the dead man's wounds began to bleed afresh.

She knew by this sign that Hagen was guilty of her husband's death, and she swore undying vengeance. She supposed that he had killed him to gain possession of his vast riches, and she determined to spoil his plan. But Hagen was as crafty as he was clever, and so he induced Brunhilda to give him the gold ring as a reward for his services to her. She knew nothing of its great value, and she hated it now because it reminded her of the false Siegfried. So she willingly gave it to Hagen, whom she considered her greatest benefactor.

No sooner had he the ring in his possession than he journeyed to Niederland, and there by its magic power he gained possession of the Rhine gold. It took him fourteen days and nights to remove the treasure from the cave on the heath. He then sunk it in the Rhine, where he intended to leave it hidden until after Kriemhild's death; but no sooner had he flung it into the river than the Rhine nymphs seized it for their own, determined to guard it so well this time that never again should their father, the God of the Rhine, have occasion to bewail its loss, and their unfaithfulness.

When Kriemhild reached Niederland, and found that the gold had been stolen from Fafner's cave, she was even more determined than before that she would be revenged upon Hagen.

10

KRIEMHILD'S REVENGE

Years passed by, and Kriemhild still mourned the loss of her noble husband. Often and often she recalled the dream that she had had in the days before Siegfried appeared in Worms. How truly her mother had interpreted its meaning!

And now she had but one wish on earth, and that was to avenge his death. She was not so beautiful as she had once been; constant tears had washed the brightness from her eyes, and her cheeks were pale.

One day there appeared in the castle a noble-looking stranger, who asked to speak with the queen. He was admitted to her presence, and she asked him his name, and also to what she owed the honor of his presence at her court.

He replied: "I am Rudiger of Bechlarn, of the court of Etzelburg. I have come hither at the request of my master, Etzel the King of the Huns, to ask your hand for him in marriage."

At first Kriemhild refused to listen to him. What had she to do with love and marriage? All the love of her heart lay buried in Siegfried's grave; all the joy of her life had vanished when he died. All that she wished for was revenge, and after that to share her dear one's tomb.

But Rudiger would not take no for an answer. Then, when he found that revenge was what she longed for, he saw his opportunity. He told her that if she would but become King Etzel's wife, he, himself, would promise to avenge her every wrong, not only those which might arise in time to come, but even those which she had suffered in the past.

Here at last was the chance she had so patiently awaited, and she eagerly seized it. She consented to become Etzel's bride, and Rudiger willingly swore undying fealty to her and her cause. And so she returned with him to Etzelburg, where the marriage was celebrated with royal pomp and ceremony.

King Etzel loved Kriemhild dearly, and was very kind to her. She was truly grateful to him, but she could not forget Siegfried, not even when a dear little son came to her. The child was named Ortlieb. And so time sped by, until the little boy's fifth birthday.

Kriemhild had now been in Etzelburg thirteen years, and in all this time she had neither seen nor heard from her home and kindred. One day she went to her husband, and told him that she was becoming ashamed of being a stranger in a foreign land without any kinspeople of her own. She said she thought it was high time that some of her family should come to visit her, and begged him to make a feast, and invite them all to be present.

Her slightest wish was Etzel's law, and so he willingly

granted her request. He at once dispatched a messenger with the invitation. Just before the messenger set out, Kriemhild went to him and told him to be sure that every one of her relatives accepted the invitation. In this way, she hoped to get her uncle Hagen within reach, without rousing any one's suspicions.

Now, when it had become known in Worms that Etzel had asked Kriemhild to marry him, Hagen had been filled with alarm. He told Gunther that it might mean great disaster for them, should Kriemhild marry Etzel, as he was one of the most powerful kings of the time.

But now thirteen years had passed, and they had neither seen nor heard from the Hunnish king and queen, and Gunther no longer feared trouble from that source. Then came Kriemhild's invitation, and for seven days it was discussed by the royal family at Worms.

Should they accept it? Gunther and his two brothers, Giselherr and Gernot, were anxious to do so, for they thought it meant that their sister wished to be at peace with her family. Gunther, particularly, was eager to be friendly, as he loved Kriemhild dearly.

Hagen alone had misgivings, and well might he dread meeting her, for he knew how sorely she had suffered at his hands. He sullenly refused to go, until Gernot at length cried out:

"I know what ails Hagen! He is thinking of Siegfried's death, and fears to go to Etzelburg."

Hagen did not wish to be thought afraid, so he consented to go, and they all prepared to accompany the messenger to Etzel's court on the following day—all except Uota, who was getting too old and feeble to leave home.

That night Uota had a dreadful dream; she thought that all the birds lay dead in the forests, and when she awoke, she hated to see her sons go, for she knew that her dream meant danger to them.

However, they set out, accompanied by one thousand brave men. On their way to Etzel's country, they came to a river that they had to cross; but they found they could not cross it on horseback, as it was swollen too high. So they had to wait until a boat should appear.

While they were waiting, they chanced to see two swan-maidens, who had come to the stream to bathe; the maidens had laid aside their feathers, and were playing about in the water like mermaids. Now Hagen knew they possessed the gift of foretelling the future, and he laid a clever plan.

When they came out of the water, they found their clothes gone, and they were very much troubled, for without their feather garments they could not fly away. Then Hagen approached them, and said he would give their feathers back if they would tell him what was to happen to the Burgundians in Etzel's land. Then one of the maidens, who cared nothing for him or his friends, and thought only of regaining her clothes, without which she could never reach her home in the sky, replied:

"Everything is fair and clear for the men of Burgundy. Sail on, sail on. You have naught to fear."

Hagen was delighted, and returned their garments with a light heart. The maidens quickly put their feathers on, and spread their wings in flight; but as they rose into the blue sky the second one cried to Hagen:

"Turn back, turn back; death and bloodshed await you in Etzelburg! Only one, of all your number, will ever live to see your native land again."

Then they disappeared in the azure depths above, and Hagen was left with a heavy heart.

At length the Burgundians secured a vessel, and embarked. They were met on the other side of the river by Dietrich von Bern, one of the lords of the Hunnish court, who greeted Hagen with these words of friendly warning:

"Kriemhild still mourns for Siegfried's loss."

But poor Hagen had no way of turning back; he had to accompany the others, whether he would or no. And sure enough, when he came into Kriemhild's presence she drew herself up haughtily, and asked:

"And pray, who invited you here, Sir Hagen? Who bid you to this feast?"

Hagen replied that he was a retainer of Gunther's, and that wherever Gunther went, he, too, must go; but her attitude and greeting showed him plainly that she had not forgiven him for his treachery.

Kriemhild greeted her brothers very cordially, and seemed rejoiced to see them, and for a few days all went well. Then came the banquet, in the midst of which in rushed Dankwart, Hagen's brother, with blood flowing

"AND, PRAY, WHO INVITED YOU HERE, SIR HAGEN?"

from a dozen wounds, and told them that the Huns had fallen upon Gunther's men and slain them all.

And immediately everything was in the wildest confusion. Protected by Rudiger, Kriemhild and Etzel escaped from the banquet hall. Then ensued a fierce battle in which all of the Huns, with the exception of Dietrich, and all the Burgundians, except Gunther and Hagen, were slain. Finally Dietrich vanquished these two, and bound them hand and foot. Then he sought Kriemhild, and made her give her word of honor that he, and he alone, should be permitted to put them to death. After that he turned the prisoners over into her keeping. She ordered them to be confined in separate dungeons.

Then she visited Hagen and sought by every means in her power to discover what he had done with the Rhine gold. This he refused to tell, saying he had taken a solemn oath never to reveal its hiding-place so long as one of his lords remained alive. Then she said that she would spare Gunther's life if Hagen would tell her where the gold was secreted.

But Hagen would not tell his secret, even to save the life of his liege lord and kinsman. And so she ordered that both of them should be beheaded, according to the custom of these olden times. And thus at last was Siegfried's death avenged by the once gentle and beautiful queen.

And of all the men of Burgundy who had crossed the water to attend King Etzel's feast, but one remained to carry the sad news back to their native land; and that was the old chaplain of Gunther's court. Everything had come to pass just as the swan-maiden had predicted. And back in Burgundy, Uota sorrowfully lived out her days with none in all that broad land to brew for her lips the cup of forgetfulness, such as she had given Siegfried. And so we must leave her alone with her sad memories.

THE END

ABOUT GRANNY'S ATTIC PRESS:

Granny's Attic searches far and wide to find antique treasures that have been forgotten. We dust them off, breathe new life, and deliver them to you. Our hope is that these old stories will give enjoyment to many generations to come.

Made in the USA
San Bernardino, CA
06 July 2014